Weekly Reader Children's Book Club presents

The Day the Fish Went Wild

The Day the Fish Went Wild

BY ELIZABETH BALDWIN HAZELTON

Illustrated by Joe Servello

CHARLES SCRIBNER'S SONS   NEW YORK

FOR JOAN AND NUNZIO

Tim's favorite fishing buddies

Chapter One

For a week, Timothy Allen had been trying to imagine what his great adventure would be. Now, suddenly, he knew. It *had* to be the spring pileup. Somehow, he would have to be out in the Sea of Cortez on a day when the fish went wild. But how was he to get there? His father couldn't help him. He would have to find a way himself.

A week ago, he'd never heard of a spring pileup or even dreamed that there was such a fantastic thing. But then, he hadn't heard of the Sea of Cortez, either —or dreamed he might be going there.

It had all started the day his father came home from the hospital. They were riding in the back seat of Grandfather Allen's car as he drove them along the freeway through the city. The traffic was heavy, and the cars, filling eight lanes of highway, were moving like two great herds of monsters, one herd crawling four abreast to the north, the other crawling four abreast to the south. On either side, tall buildings hemmed them in like the walls of a canyon, and above them, the sky was a low, gray ceiling of smog.

But Tim was too happy to take much notice of the crawling cars and the depressing skies. For him, only one thing was important: his father was sitting in the seat beside him, well enough to come home. He didn't look very strong, leaning back against the pillows the nurse had put behind him, but that didn't matter. After the long weeks of separation while he'd been in the hospital, just having him there was wonderful.

"The Doc was right," his father said suddenly.

Tim waited to hear what the doctor was right about, but instead, his father said, "Look at them!"

"The cars?" Tim asked.

"The drivers—sitting behind their steering wheels like men in cages."

Tim and his grandfather looked at the men in the cars on both sides of them. It was true—they did look caged.

"See those grim faces?" his father said. "It's the same in all the cars. Hundreds of people with no joy in them."

"I guess they're all mad because the traffic is so slow," Tim said.

"That's it. They're all tied up in knots, worrying about every second of time they're losing. The Doc was right: we're all slaves of clocks and calendars.

But d'you know something, Son? You and I are going to break out of bondage."

"We are?"

"Tim, how would you like to go on a trip with me?"

"Oh boy, would I! Where to, Dad?"

"Mexico. Not the part of it where all the tourists go, but the wild, primitive country few Americans have ever seen."

"Have you seen it, Dad?"

"Yes, I was down there, once, before you were born." He addressed Grandpa Allen, in the front seat. "Remember that, Dad?"

Intent on his driving, Grandpa nodded. "Scientific expedition, wasn't it?"

"Right—and my job was to write a feature story about it for my newspaper. From all I hear, it hasn't changed much in the years since."

"What's it like?" asked Tim.

"It's a long peninsula that reaches down into the tropics, with a coast as rugged and beautiful as anything in the world and a great sea full of islands that no one has ever touched foot on."

"Wow!"

"And the best part of it is, it's not far away."

Tim's heart flipped inside his chest. The way his father spoke, it all sounded real—yet how could it be? He was barely strong enough to come home. How could he go on a trip *anywhere?* Maybe it was just wishful thinking—like some of the places they'd talked about when Tim had sat by his father's bed during visiting hours.

"We don't have much money," Mr. Allen went on, "and we won't have until I can get back on the job, but living down there is cheap. Why, you can almost feed us yourself, Tim, with the fish you can catch."

"Dad—" Tim could hardly bear to ask the question, for fear he was wrong. "Dad, is this for real?"

His father looked at him in amazement. "Great Scott, Tim, you mean you thought—"

"I mean, it's not just something to think about?" Tim said. "You really are well enough to go?"

"That's how I'm going to *get* well, Son. Doctor's orders. He said, 'Throw away the clocks and the calendar and get out into the wilderness.' So that's what I'm going to do, Tim. How about it? D'you want to go with me?"

"Do I!" Tim exclaimed. "Holy Smoke, Dad, you bet I do!"

"Then it's a deal." His father reached for his hand and gripped it tightly. "When we get to Grandpa's house, we'll take out the map and plot our course."

When Grandma Allen had his father comfortably installed in a lounging chair on the lanai, with a pot of hot coffee on the table beside him, they began to study the map of the peninsula in Mexico known as Baja—or Lower—California. Tim saw that it was a

long, narrow tongue of land with a range of mountains extending down the middle of it. On the west it was bounded by the Pacific Ocean. But it was the eastern coast that was important to him—the coast that bordered the Gulf of California, sometimes called by the name the early Spanish explorers gave it, the Sea of Cortez.

"Look here," his father said, pointing to an area about one-third down the length of the peninsula. "See all these indentations? They're bays with broad beaches of white sand and the bluest water you've ever set eyes on. And the fishing! Tim, I won't even try to tell you about it, because you won't believe it until you see it. But I can guarantee you that, one way or another, the Sea of Cortez will bring you the greatest adventure of your life."

A thrill of anticipation ran along Tim's spine. He felt as if he couldn't get there fast enough.

"Is this where we're going, Dad?" he asked. "To these bays?"

"To this one right here." His father pointed out a deep indentation sheltered by an island. "There's a little fishing village on the beach, with no more than one hundred inhabitants, probably counting burros and dogs." He grinned. "We'll bring it up to one hundred and two."

"You mean we're really going to live there?"

"Until I get well. After that, maybe we'll explore some of the other bays."

"Yee-ouw!" Tim shouted. "How're we going to get there? By boat?"

"I don't think so," Mr. Allen said thoughtfully. "We'd have to hire a small cruiser at the head of the Gulf. That would be pretty costly. And there are some dangerous stretches of sea between anchorages. It would take a more experienced skipper than I am to risk those savage winds and currents."

"But golly, Dad, I don't see any roads," protested Tim. "At least not any good ones."

"There aren't any good ones, Son. In fact, they're probably the worst roads on the whole continent," his father said emphatically, "but that's just the way we want them."

"It is?"

"You bet—because that's what keeps the country primitive. If the roads were good, those beaches would be crowded with tourists. But as long as they're bad, they'll belong to the fishermen who live there with their families—and to a few hardy adventurers, like us."

Mr. Allen poured himself another cup of coffee, and Tim saw that his hand shook from the effort of holding the heavy pot. He wasn't very "hardy" yet, Tim thought.

"No ordinary car could make it over those ruts and rocks," his father went on, "but we could trade in the old jalopy for a jeep with four-wheel drive."

"I'd like that," Tim said. "A jeep would be great."

"I'd like it too, Son. I'd like to take on those narrow, precipitous roads through the wilderness. It would be a real challenge. But there's one catch: we'd have to wait two or three months, until I could get back my strength."

"Sure, Dad!" Tim said. "You've got to be careful for a long time. I understand that. We can wait."

"We can, Tim," his father said, "but I don't want to, and neither do you!"

"No, sir—"

"Then that eliminates the jeep—but look at this." His father pointed out a small rectangular mark on the map, beside the bay. "That's an airport. Not for big airliners. It's just an area scraped flat, behind the beach, but it's good enough for small private planes."

"Gosh, Dad, d'you mean we can fly in?"

"Exactly. There's a fellow just across the border who flies passengers down in his four-seater. Grandpa can drive us to that point, and I figure if we can get a flight, we can take off in about a week."

"The only place *you'll* go, in a week, is back to the hospital, if you don't rest!" warned Grandma Allen, bustling in from the kitchen. "Put away that map, Timmie, and help me get your father to bed."

Tim had been so intent on plans for the journey that he hadn't noticed how pale his father was. He folded the map quickly and lent his shoulder for support, as Mr. Allen walked to the bedroom. Feeling his father's weight, Tim wondered if he could possibly be strong enough to undertake the journey in a week.

Perhaps his father sensed his doubt, for he winked and said, "Don't let Grandma fool you, Son. With you to help me, I'll make it."

Chapter Two

Tim helped in every way he could. With his grandfather, he went to a sporting goods store to buy new camping gear and fishing tackle. With his grandmother, he went to the market to pick out the canned goods and grocery staples they would need to supplement the food they would take from the sea. And he delivered the letter that Mr. Allen wrote to the principal of his school, explaining where Tim was going to be and arranging to take along his textbooks so he could study part of the time and keep up with his class.

Through it all, he kept a close watch on his father. Every afternoon, they took a walk together, and each day they went a little farther than the day before. Each day his father seemed a bit stronger, but as the time for departure neared, Tim was afraid that he wouldn't be strong enough. He lay awake at night, worrying about it, because now that everything was ready, the thought of having to postpone their trip was more than he could bear.

The journey was the only hazard; he felt sure of that. Once his father got to the bay in Mexico, he could lie on the warm sand and soak up the sunshine and fresh air. Tim could catch all the fish they needed, and he could make fires and cook them, too. His father had taught him how to do that when they had fished the lakes and streams of the High Sierras. He was older now—almost eleven—old enough to do it by himself, if they could just get there.

On the evening before the morning of departure, Tim and his grandfather packed all the gear into the trunk of the car. That night, it was harder than ever for him to go to sleep. His pulse raced with excitement, as he lay in the darkness thinking of his father. "Please," he whispered, "let him be strong in the morning. Please, make him able to go!"

A firm touch on his shoulder woke him. Opening his eyes, he saw his father bending over him. The first rays of the sun, slanting through the window, told him it was morning.

"Dad," he said anxiously, sitting up, "are you okay?"

"You bet!" His father's smile was bright and confident. "How about you?"

"Great!" Tim said, swinging his feet over the side of the bed.

"Then jet out of here and get washed and dressed. It's almost time to leave."

Riding along the freeway, Tim couldn't recall eating breakfast, though he knew he had. All he could think of was: *we're on our way!*

With Grandfather Allen at the wheel and Grandma in the front seat beside him, they sped southward along the highway toward the border town of Tijuana, Mexico, where the small plane was waiting. To Tim, the long drive seemed endless, but at last they reached the United States border and passed through customs. From there it was only a short distance to the Tijuana airport. Once we're on the plane, Tim thought, nothing can stop us!

The plane was a single-engined four-seater, which meant there was room for only three passengers and the Mexican pilot. The other passenger, an American sport fisherman, was already there. The camping gear and supplies were quickly stowed away, and the plane was ready for takeoff.

"Remember, Tim, you're in charge," said his grandfather, gripping his shoulders. "If you need any help, get on the ship-to-shore radio down there and call us."

"Yes, sir," Tim said, "but I won't need any. We'll be fine."

When his grandmother had given him a goodbye hug, Tim and his father climbed into their seats and fastened their safety belts. There was a roar of the motor, warming up, and the plane began to taxi down the strip. Moments later they were airborne, and Tim's grandparents were little figures waving from the ground below.

Tim had been so eager to get underway that he hadn't had time to think of anything else, but as the plane soared higher and the ground dropped farther and farther away, he felt a sinking sensation in the pit of his stomach. He had flown in a huge airliner once, when he was younger, but this was very different. The plane, vibrating with the roar of its one engine, seemed very small and frail, like a bird fighting the turbulent air. He gripped the arms of his seat hard, and the muscles of his whole body were tight, as if he were trying by his own strength to hold the aircraft steady in the sky.

His father noticed his tension, and leaned across the aisle, smiling. "We're bucking a headwind, but don't worry, Son. Our pilot will get us there."

Tim loosened his hold on the chair. "It feels different from the big ones," he said, by way of explanation.

"You bet it does," said Mr. Allen. "A lot more scary."

It wasn't scary to his father, Tim thought. Nothing was. He felt embarrassed and ashamed that his father should have seen that he was scared.

"Take a look at those mountains," his father was saying. "That's the San Pedro Mártir range—solid granite, with peaks as high as ten thousand feet."

Tim stood up to look out the window on his father's side. Range on range of rugged, desolate mountains stretched as far to the east as he could see. No town, no village—just barren wilderness. The sight of it didn't make him any more comfortable.

He settled back into his seat and looked out of his own window. Beneath him lay the western coast of Baja California. Never before had he seen, from the sky, how land and water met. It seemed a little unreal, like a painting: bright, curving beaches and jutting headlands edged with foaming white breakers that looked like lace.

Beyond the breakers lay the deep and limitless blue waters of the Pacific Ocean, reaching all the way to the horizon. Tim wondered what it would be like to be in a plane that crashed into the ocean. His father knew. He had been a pilot in the Air Force, and he had been flying alone in a jet when it happened. Another plane had collided with him over a big city. The other pilot had parachuted to safety seconds before his plane crashed into a building and burst into flames, endangering the lives of many people. Tim's father knew that if he, too, bailed out, many more might be killed. So he stayed with his plane and rode it out over the city to the sea. A fisherman in a small cruiser had saved his life, but he'd been in the hospital many times since then because of his injuries.

Tim wondered what he would have done if he'd been in his father's place. He wanted to believe that he would have stayed with the plane, but in his heart he wasn't sure.

It was hard, sometimes, to think about how brave his father was—especially at a moment like this, when he had been scared just riding in this little plane. Maybe it would be different if he were at the controls. If he were the pilot, he'd know what he was doing. He hoped it would be different, because it would be awful to find out that he was a coward, especially with such a father.

He thought about the promised adventure in the Sea of Cortez and wondered if it would be something frightening.

After a while, his father leaned toward him to tell him about the country beneath them—how it had changed very little in the four hundred years since the Spanish explorers had first set foot on it, except that in that long-ago time there had been thousands of primitive Indians living along its coasts. The Jesuit priests had come to convert the Indians and put them to work building missions along the whole length of the peninsula. But now nearly all of the Indians were gone, many of the missions had fallen into ruins, and the country was almost as wild as it had been before the Spaniards came.

Time passed quickly for Tim as he watched the land that seemed to be flowing beneath them—a great empty wilderness stretching between two seas.

"How about all that space?" his father said. "No buildings down there to close us in—and up here, nothing but clear blue skies all the way to the stars."

"A person would sure be alone down there," Tim said.

"It's good for a man to be alone with nature sometimes," his father said. "Gives him a chance to find out who he is."

"Doesn't everybody know who he is?" Tim asked.

"Not always—not the real *inside* who."

Like me? Tim wondered. Like not knowing whether I'm a coward or not? But he didn't ask his father.

They were over a high plateau and the vast expanse of an ancient lake bed that was dry as a desert. The pilot turned the little plane eastward, and they flew over miles of granite ridges cut into fantastic shapes by the winds that had blown across them in times of ferocious storms. Between them were narrow canyons too steep to climb, and scattered in their depths were huge boulders that looked as if they had been shaken from the mountain tops by some violent earthquake. Then suddenly the towering

ridges dropped away, and beyond them Tim saw the
brilliant blue of the Sea of Cortez.

"There it is, Son!" his father said. "The greatest
fishbowl in the world!"

Tim's heart pounded at the sight of it, and he
pressed his face against the window, straining to see
the off-shore islands with their high cliffs and rocky
promontories. Losing altitude, the aircraft swung
out beyond the coastline, and as it turned, Tim saw
the sparkling waters of the bay, held within a great
curving arm of land. Riding gently on its surface
were boats of many sizes.

At the head of the bay, directly beneath a mountain peak, the little village lay in a grove of palms. The plane skimmed over an island, startling thousands of nesting seabirds who rose up in shrieking protest, then touched down smoothly on the airstrip behind the beach.

As it taxied to a stop, Tim shouted, "Dad, we made it! We're here!"

"We sure are," said his father, smiling happily. "How does it look to you?"

"It looks great!" Tim declared excitedly. "Absolutely great!"

Chapter Three

They had barely had time to climb out of their seats when the plane was surrounded by all the men and boys of the village who were not out fishing. Their bronzed faces were cheerful and friendly, and it was easy to see that the arrival of strangers was an event of importance.

Capable hands were quick to help the pilot lift out their gear and load it into wheelbarrows, and soon Tim and his father and the other passenger were walking to the settlement, escorted by the good-natured Mexicans. A broad-shouldered man with thick black hair and bushy eyebrows came to greet them with a welcoming smile. He introduced himself as Señor Moreno, and after he had talked to Mr. Allen, he led them to a little house with a palm-thatched roof.

"It is all right, no?" he asked, raising his eyebrows in concern.

"It's fine, Señor Moreno," said Mr. Allen.

"You bet!" Tim declared enthusiastically.

Señor Moreno smiled his wide, warm smile again and nodded happily, as if it were important to him that the little house should please them. The men who had followed with the wheelbarrow smiled, too. They unloaded the gear and put it on the hard earthen floor of the house, and then, refusing any payment for their help, they drifted away regretfully, as though they'd like to have stayed longer, if they could have thought of any excuse.

But even with the men gone, a little circle of interested spectators still remained, all of them Mexican boys in patched shorts and shirts who needed no more reason to linger than friendly curiosity.

"I am Pancho Ramirez," said one of them. He was about Tim's age, with a mop of curly black hair and black eyes shining with excitement. "My mother says you will come to eat with us. See?" He indicated the woven-palm house next door, where a Mexican lady with a bright flowered scarf around her head was cooking in her outdoor kitchen. "Already she has

made for you, special, the chicken with tomatoes and chilies."

"*Sí!* You come now!" called Señora Ramirez. She motioned them to come and sit at a table at the edge of the beach, under a palm-thatched roof. "It is ready —and you have the hunger, no?"

"We have the hunger, yes!" Mr. Allen said. "Am I right, *compañero?*"

"I'll say!" said Tim, who was feeling ravenous. "But what is *'compañero'?*"

"It means pal—or companion," his father explained.

"Hey!" said Tim, impressed. "I like that!"

"Okay, *compañero,* let's accept the Señora's kind invitation."

Pancho and his younger brother, Lino, followed Tim and his father to the house of the Señora, while the other boys of the village straggled away as regretfully as had their elders.

"My house is yours," the Señora said as she led them to the table. Her suntanned face was handsome, and Tim noticed that her eyes were as shining as Pancho's. "You know already my Pancho and Lino," she said, "and this is Mariquita."

Mariquita was in the kitchen making tortillas. She was older than Tim—perhaps fifteen—and her smile was shy, but her dark eyes were sparkling. It seemed odd to Tim that here in this Mexican village where he and his father were strangers, everyone was glad to see them. It gave him a warm feeling—like a family reunion.

They sat at the table and looked across the white sand to the glistening blue waters of the bay, while Señora Ramirez served heaping platefuls of stewed chicken and frijoles, and Mariquita went on making the delicious-smelling tortillas, one after another.

A line of dugout canoes lay on the beach, and Tim saw that another was coming in from the bay, paddled by a man and a boy. As it touched the shore, both jumped out to pull it up beyond the water's edge. When they had drawn it far enough, the man lifted out a very large fish and handed it to the boy, who began to drag it up the beach while his companion lifted out a second one.

Tim longed to see the fish, but his father looked very tired, and he knew he should stay and help him unpack. The Señora noticed his weariness, too.

"You will rest here, Señor Allen," she commanded, indicating a hammock hung between pillars made of palm trunks. "Mariquita and I, we will unpack for you."

Tim's father tried to protest, but the Señora was insistent. "The little house you have rented, it was the house of my son and his wife before they went to La Paz," she said, "so it is for us to make it comfortable for you."

"I can help," Tim volunteered.

"*Sí*—later," agreed the Señora, "but now it is the

fish you want to see, no? So go, *vamos!*"

Tim looked questioningly at his father.

"You've got your orders," Mr. Allen said, with a grin. *"Vamos*—and find out what's to be caught for dinner!"

Tim was underway before his father had finished speaking, with Pancho keeping pace and Lino trailing behind them. A little group of watchers had already gathered around the boy with the fish, and hungry seagulls and huge black ravens from the mountains were flying greedily overhead, hoping for a share of the catch.

When Tim reached the circle of men and boys, he let out a breathless "Wow!" The pugnacious-looking fish with the blunt head and the yellow tail was the biggest one he had ever seen.

"You think this is big?" asked the boy who was holding it.

"I'll say!" gasped Tim, still out of breath.

"It is nothing," declared the boy scornfully. "From the shore, I can catch bigger."

The boy was a year or two older than Tim, of thicker build, with swarthy skin and straight black hair. The look on his face was as aggressive as that of his fish.

"How big is this one?" Tim asked.

"Maybe forty pounds. But last week I cast from the beach, and caught one of fifty."

"I saw the *toro* you caught from the beach," challenged Pancho, "and it was maybe half the size of this one."

"So—you call me a liar!" declared the boy belligerently.

"No, Rodrigo," said an old man with a kindly face beneath a wide sombrero. "Pancho says only that the fish grows larger with each telling. It is the way of fish."

"I have caught many you have not seen!" Rodrigo told Pancho. "Were you in the boat when I hooked the great grouper? Did you see me catch him?"

"I have heard it was not you who caught him, but he who caught you!" Pancho replied.

There was a burst of laughter from the little circle of watchers.

"*Si!*" shouted Lino. "It was you who went into the water—not he who came out!"

"I would like to see any of you bring in a two-hundred-pound fish!" Rodrigo declared angrily.

"Two hundred pounds!" Tim exclaimed. "You must be kidding!"

"The two hundred pounds is possible," Pancho admitted, "but to hook him is one thing—to deck him is another!"

"You mean there really are fish out there that weigh two hundred pounds?" Tim demanded.

"There is a *mero* that weighs one thousand," Pancho told him.

Tim let out a long whistle of amazement.

"And the marlin *azul*," said the old man, "he may weigh two thousand."

"The devilray," declared Rodrigo, "can be twice two thousand!"

Tim looked to Pancho for confirmation.

"It is true," Pancho nodded, "there are many great fish out in the sea beyond the islands."

"If I went out there, could I see them?" Tim asked.

"If you went out in a cruiser or on the charter boat, you might see some," Pancho told him. "The devilrays, maybe, or the big sharks. The great game-fish, too, if it should happen that the Americano sport fishermen would catch them."

"If there was a spring pileup," said Lino, "he would see them all."

"*Sí, sí*. He would see them all then," agreed the other boys, their eyes widening at the thought.

"What's a spring pileup?" Tim asked.

"It is a thing of danger!" Rodrigo declared. "And no place for a coward!"

"Who's a coward?" Pancho demanded, bristling.

"I have not said *who* is a coward," Rodrigo insisted, backing down. "How would I know what your Americano is? I have only said a coward should not go to the pileup."

"Have you seen it?" Tim asked.

"*Sí*, many times," Rodrigo bragged. "It is a great thing to see—for one who is brave!"

"It is not wise to talk too much of bravery," the old man said gently, "for beneath the talk may be a man who is afraid."

"I am never afraid," Rodrigo declared sullenly, dragging his big fish on up the beach.

Suddenly Lino let out an excited whoop, and the watchers turned to see a big fishing boat coming to anchor in the bay.

"It is *La Hechicera*, the charter boat!" Pancho exclaimed. "Maybe they have caught some of the great fish!"

The men hurried off to get their wheelbarrows, and the boys ran down to the water's edge to wait for the skiffs from the big boat. Rodrigo abandoned his fish on the sand to run after them.

"His fish—" Tim said, "what's the name of it?"

"We call it *'toro,'*" Pancho said, "but the Americanos name it jack crevalle. It is good for eating."

"Is it true that we could catch one from the shore?"

"Sí—if we were lucky," Pancho admitted, "but we will do better in the canoe. We will take the dugout of my brother, but first let us see what the Americano sport fishermen have caught."

Out in the bay, the crew of the charter boat had lowered five skiffs, and now they were loading them with the day's catch. Even from a distance, Tim could see that there were a great many fish.

"They have been out three days," Pancho told him. "It could be they were in a pileup."

"Pancho," Tim said thoughtfully, as they walked down the beach, "was Rodrigo telling the truth? Is the pileup a thing of danger?"

"If you fall into the sea in the middle of it, it is a thing of death," Pancho answered, "but even in the skiff, it is a thing of terror."

"Have you seen it?"

Pancho nodded. "Once, when I was small. I was with my father and uncle in the canoe, far out in the bay, when all around us the sea began to boil."

"Boil?"

"With fishes. My father commanded me to lie down in the canoe so I would not fall in and be eaten."

"There were fish big enough to eat you?"

"Big enough to eat a man!" Pancho insisted. "In a pileup, all sizes are there—big and small and medium. And all go wild. They will eat anything. Even the great sharks eat each other. It is frightening to see, but also, it is the most exciting thing in the world!"

Tim was silent. He didn't know what would happen to him if he were in a skiff when a pileup started—whether he would be a coward or brave—but he knew he had to be there. The spring pileup had to be his great adventure.

"Have you never seen it since?" he asked.

"No," Pancho said, "but I would like to."

"Wouldn't you be afraid?"

"*Si,* I would!" Pancho admitted. "On *La Hechicera,* my brother Alfaro is cook, and he has seen Americanos turn white when the pileup happened. Some even command the guides to get them out of it, pronto. Big men, they are, and not often afraid. Me?" Pancho shrugged. "I would be afraid for sure, but I would like to go."

"Me, too," Tim said earnestly.

"For you, there is a good chance," Pancho declared. "Your father is rich Americano. He can rent a small cruiser."

"How much is it?" Tim asked doubtfully.

"Fifty dollars for each day."

"Fifty dollars!" said Tim, stricken.

"*Si.*"

"It might as well be one hundred—or a thousand!"

"Your father does not have the fifty dollars?" asked Pancho in surprise.

"Not for renting cruisers," Tim said dejectedly. "We need every dollar to live on."

Pancho was puzzled. "I have thought all Americanos were rich," he said. "The ones I have seen— the sport fishermen—they fly down in airplanes of their own, and they come only to rent the boats and go out for the gamefish."

"My father didn't come for the fishing," Tim explained. "He's been sick in the hospital for a long time. He came to lie in the sun and get well."

"It is a good place for sun," Pancho agreed.

"There is almost no day without it."

"What about the charter boat?" Tim asked. "Does it cost a lot to get on that, too?"

"*Sí*. I think very many dollars. But it goes out only when it is chartered by the rich Americanos—and the men who sail on it, they do not take strangers with them."

"But I've got to go!" Tim insisted. "There has to be a way!"

"We will think of something," Pancho promised.

There was a roar of motors as the outboard skiffs started for the shore. The men of the village were pushing their empty wheelbarrows down the beach, and the boys were already plunging into the water.

"Quick!" commanded Pancho. "We will meet a skiff and maybe earn a dollar."

Pancho raced into the water, and Tim waded in beside him. The skiffs sped toward them, their motors cutting off as they neared the beach. Even before they scraped the sand, there was a wild splashing and yelling as the boys shouted, "Let me carry your fish, Señor! For one American dollar, I will carry and clean your fish!"

The villagers began to lift out the fish—most of them larger than the jack—and pile them into wheelbarrows. It was then that Tim saw the immense fish lying in the bottom of the skiff nearest him. It was almost true, what Rodrigo had said, that the jack was nothing compared to this one. It was very long—

much longer than Tim was tall—with a dozen gray stripes across its back and an upper jaw that extended far out like a narrow spear.

"The striped marlin!" exclaimed Pancho. "We will carry it for you, Señor—my friend and I will carry it!"

"You'll need several friends to carry that one," said the angler, who had just jumped out of the skiff.

"We'll help you, Pancho!" declared one of the boatmen.

"Okay, Señor?" asked Pancho.

"Okay, General," said the American. "You've got yourself a deal."

The boatmen were already hoisting the huge fish out of the skiff, and a moment later it lay on the sand with a rope stretched under it, where the wedge-shaped body was thickest.

"Tim, you will hold the spear with me," Pancho ordered, "and Lino, you and Tomaso carry the tail."

As Tim moved toward the head of the marlin, Rodrigo appeared suddenly from behind him and with a rough shove pushed him aside.

"You are not of the village—you are rich Americano," he declared. "You have no right to carry the fish." He took hold of the creature's beak. "I will carry it for you, Señor," he told the fisherman.

"You will get your own fish!" Pancho shouted angrily, breaking Rodrigo's hold on the beak. "We have got already a deal."

"That's right," agreed the American. "You're too late, buddy."

"*Vamos!*" growled one of the boatmen, pushing Rodrigo aside.

The two men took their places, one on each side of the monster, and each grasped an end of rope in his hand. Pancho and Tim gripped the long spear, and Lino and Tomaso took hold of the tail. The marlin seemed enormously heavy, and Tim wondered how they could possibly move it anywhere.

"Now—*vamanos!*" shouted the boatman, and all six of them lifted at once. Slowly they moved up the beach, the great fish's belly dragging on the sand. At length, they reached the weighing frame. Other villagers came to help, and together they hoisted the marlin up with ropes.

"For the Americanos," Pancho whispered, "it is not important to catch the fish for food, but only to see how big he is!"

"Four hundred pounds!" gasped Tim, watching the scale. "Wow! That's some *big!*"

The proud angler pulled a roll of greenbacks out of his pocket, and when he had passed several to the boatman, he peeled off four more and gave them to Pancho—one for each boy.

"Okay, General?" he asked.

"*Sí*, okay *bueno!*" exclaimed Pancho happily. He handed one dollar to Lino and one to Tomaso, and as he handed Tim the third, he whispered, "With

such a fish, the Americanos give much money. Maybe if we meet all the skiffs of the sport fishermen, we can earn together enough to rent a cruiser."

"Yeah!" Tim agreed excitedly. "Already we've got two. That leaves only forty-eight to go."

Chapter Four

But earning the other forty-eight was not as easy as Tim and Pancho had hoped. The American sport fishermen who flew down to the bay came on weekends, and the arrival of the small planes became as important and exciting to Tim as it was to the boys of the village. Once in a while, a plane swooped down out of the empty sky on Friday, but usually the fishermen came on Saturday and Tim and Pancho met them as the villagers had met him and his father.

Sometimes there were only one or two passengers in the little single-engined aircraft, occasionally there were four. And once there was a real luxury plane with two engines and eight passengers. Tim and Pancho always counted the number of arriving anglers, for each one was a potential client. There was a chance that each man might catch one of the great fish and, in his joy and excitement, pay generously for the carrying and cleaning.

The problem was that relatively few fishermen came, and for each one there were many boys, all of them eagerly hoping to collect some of the American dollars. And each had a right to his share.

From Monday to Friday, there was no chance at all to earn. The little village lay quiet and dreaming under the baking hot sun, with almost no intrusion from the outer world. On a rare day, a small plane might land briefly on its flight to the cities of Loreto and La Paz, to the south; or there might be the excitement of a supply truck laboring in over the mountains after its three-day ordeal on the dreadful roads from the west coast city of Ensenada, to the north. But the charter boat and the little fleet of cruisers and skiffs rode quietly at anchor in the bay. Only the villagers went out in their canoes to bring in the daily catch of fish, lobsters, and crabs that fed their families; and on some days, the turtle boat went out—or returned.

The children of the village attended the small school, while Tim studied under his father's tutelage, to keep up with his own classmates on the American side of the border. As soon as school was out, he and Pancho swam in the warm waters of the bay or paddled out in the canoe to fish.

It was a double-ended canoe, carved from a single log and covered inside and out with a thin layer of plaster, to make it waterproof. As the boys paddled out from shore, one of them at each end, they could see thousands of minnows in the clear green water. The tiniest ones crowded into the shallows to escape the next largest size, who were safe only in slightly deeper water. As the canoe glided farther out, the size of the fish increased with the depth of the water, and when they were several hundred yards from shore, Tim and Pancho baited their hooks and cast out their lines.

But on this particular day, Tim's thoughts were less on his fishing than on the spring pileup. "In three weekends, we've made only seven dollars and a half, between us," he declared dejectedly. "That means we still need forty-two dollars and fifty cents."

"It is a lot of money," Pancho agreed.

"My father will be well and leaving here before we ever make it, carrying fish. If only there was some other way we could earn . . ."

"*Si*—but for boys, there is nothing."

Tim knew it was true. Even for men, there were only two ways of earning. Some of the villagers, like Pancho's father, went out in the turtle boat to harpoon the great sea turtles and bring them back to the pen at the water's edge, where they were kept until they could be transported to the mainland or to Ensenada, where they were sold. Others, like Pancho's brother, Alfaro, worked as crew or guides on the charter boat or the cruisers of Señor Moreno. It was he who owned the little fleet of boats and the guest cabins at the edge of the beach, where the sport fishermen stayed.

"Here, it is not important to have money," Pancho explained. "My father says, to have a house and plenty of fish to eat—this is enough—and the men of the village all think like him. To do a little work for a little money is good, he says, but there is no need for much work—or much money."

"Except to rent a cruiser."

"*Sí*—except for that," Pancho conceded sadly.

While the boys pondered their problem in silence, a long wedge of pelicans soared over them, flapping and sailing in unison as they searched for fish. Sud-

denly, as Tim watched, they folded their wings and dove headlong into the water. When they came up, they emptied the seawater they had scooped into the pouches beneath their beaks and swallowed their catch of fish before the gulls could steal them. Then they flapped heavily upward with their powerful wings and began coasting over the bay again, to resume their fishing.

"*La Hechicera* is chartered for this weekend," said Pancho, breaking the silence. "There will be many anglers—perhaps fifteen or twenty. They go out before the sun rises tomorrow, and for two days."

"Golly, I wish we were going with them!"

"Tim, I have been thinking," said Pancho slowly. "There is one way we could go."

"There is?" Tim stared at Pancho in amazement. "How?" he demanded.

"We could stow away."

"Stow away!" Tim's eyes widened as he took in the idea.

"*Sí*. It is true, what you said about the money," Pancho admitted. "We will never make it in time. Even if your father should stay, the big pileups will be over."

"Over? What d'you mean?"

"They happen only in the time of the spring migrations, when the great schools of yellowtail and other fish come up from the south, into the cooler waters at this end of the sea," Pancho explained. "It is when the hungry big fish come upon the thousands of little fish that the wildness begins."

"Then if we don't stow away now, I'll never see one!" declared Tim, with shocked realization.

Pancho nodded. "But if we do, there is still a chance."

For a long moment, Tim gazed at Pancho, hardly aware of seeing him, while his mind explored the situation. "If we're caught," he said at last, "what will happen?"

"Then"—Pancho shrugged—"we will be in trouble."

"What will they do to us?"

"Who knows? The *capitán* is the father of Rodrigo, and a man of hot temper. If he finds us before the boat passes the island of the sea lions, he may throw us overboard."

"You're kidding!"

"No. He will think we can swim to the rocks and wait till the boat returns."

"But you said it would be out two days."

"And I said, also, he has the hot temper."

"But we wouldn't have anything to eat or drink!"

"We could find some food of the sea and eat it raw. In two days we would not die."

"We could carry some food on us, in plastic bags," Tim said, already reaching for a solution to the potential problem, "but what about the sea lions? Would they attack us?"

"I am not sure," Pancho admitted, "but I think there would be more danger in the currents around the island."

"Gosh!" Tim whispered. "Do you really think he'd throw us over?"

"If Rodrigo had anything to say, he would."

"Rodrigo? What's he got to do with it?"

"He will be on board. When there are many anglers, he gets the job of helping Alfaro in the galley."

"Oh, wow!" Tim groaned. "Then we *are* sunk."

"But not if we are not found before the island of the sea lions," Pancho insisted. "Once we are past that, to throw us overboard would be to kill us, and I think his temper is not *that* hot."

"Golly Moses! I hope not!"

"Past the island, we may be in trouble, but we will be aboard, and if there is a pileup, there is a chance that we will see it."

"There's a chance we'll be in irons, down in the hold."

Pancho shrugged again. "I agree it is not the best way to go, but I think it is the only way."

Tim was silent, weighing the odds. It seemed unlikely that the captain, no matter how evil his temper, would seriously endanger their lives. After all, Pancho's brother, Alfaro, would be on board. Punished, they might be—and severely—if they were caught. But there was a chance they might not be. At least, at this moment, the danger was only a vague shadow, while the excitement of a pileup was a shining promise. To stow away would make it a double adventure.

"Maybe it is better if we forget it," Pancho suggested gloomily.

"No!" Tim declared, with sudden decision. "Let's do it!"

"*Bueno!* We will not think of the trouble but only of the fun!" He began to retrieve his neglected line, from which the bait had long since been stolen, and Tim followed suit.

"If she sails in the morning, we don't have much time," Tim said. "What do we do first?"

"We go aboard and search for a good hiding place."

"When?"

"Maybe now."

"But some of the crew are on board," Tim protested. "I can see them from here."

"*Sí.* All day they have been preparing her to sail, but I think soon they will go ashore to eat."

Pancho laid his pole in the bottom of the canoe and picked up a paddle. With a few deft strokes, he swung the dugout around until it was pointed toward the charter boat, lying at anchor some three hundred yards away.

"We will move in close," he said. "Then when the men leave, we'll be ready to climb aboard, pronto."

"What about the other boys that are fishing in the bay? Won't they spot us? Rodrigo's there, with his little brother."

"*Sí*," Pancho admitted thoughtfully. "From him, there could be trouble."

Chapter Five

Tim laid his pole beside Pancho's and settled into the opposite end of the canoe. Dipping their paddles in rhythm, they glided through the water. As they approached the big boat, Tim could make out the letters of her name on the bow: *La Hechicera del Mar.* He knew the meaning of the words; his father had translated them for him. *La Hechicera* meant "the sorceress," and *del Mar,* "of the sea."

"Why is she named 'The Sorceress of the Sea'?" Tim asked.

"Alfaro says it is because she has a power over the waves, like a witch. In a storm, when other boats founder, she rides safely through. He says it has always been so. Before she was converted to a boat for fishing, she was a vessel for air and sea rescues, and then, too, she came always safely to harbor."

"She must be a lucky boat."

"*Sí,* I think very lucky."

"Gosh, I hope she'll be lucky for us."

"Look!" Pancho exclaimed. "Already the luck begins!"

On the deck of *La Hechicera* the men had completed their duties and were climbing down the ladder to the skiff tied alongside. The outboard motor started with a roar, and they sped toward the beach.

"We'll need more luck than that," Tim declared. "Rodrigo's watching us."

"Let's drop anchor here," Pancho said, "and pretend to swim away from *La Hechicera.*"

When the anchor had splashed down, the boys slipped over the side. The water felt warm and silky against Tim's skin, and as he stroked away from the charter boat, a throng of brightly-colored fishes finned through the clear blue depths beneath him, but he barely noticed them. His mind was on Rodrigo—and the fact that time was running out. The deckhands had gone ashore, but there was no telling when someone else might come out to board *La Hechicera,* and the sun was already slipping down behind the mountains. If he and Pancho were not ashore in time for supper, the "trouble" would come long before they could get around to stowing away.

As Tim raised his head to check on Rodrigo, Pancho pulled alongside to mutter, "He's coming over!"

"What'll we do?"

"Keep swimming—and see what happens."

When they had put another twenty yards between them and the big boat, they paused to tread water.

Rodrigo and his brother were still coming toward them. They had almost reached the dugout when Tim heard a distant roar of motors and a small plane zoomed down over the mountains, followed a moment later by another.

Rodrigo heard it, too, and stopped paddling.

"The fishermen!" Pancho shouted.

Rodrigo paused, torn between his curiosity and the impending landing of the aircraft.

"Swim for the dugout, pronto!" Pancho commanded, as he started for it with long lunging strokes.

Tim plunged after him, and seeing them coming, Rodrigo made a swift decision. With a sharp command to his brother, he began to paddle mightily for shore.

When Tim came up for air alongside the dugout, Pancho was already clinging to the gunwale. "It worked!" he said. "He thinks he's racing us to the landing strip."

"Then let's go, before he finds out he isn't!" Tim gasped. Sucking in air, he jackknifed under and swam for *La Hechicera,* with Pancho following him.

When the dark shape of the hull loomed ahead of him, Tim surfaced and filled his lungs. Rodrigo's dugout was still slicing toward the beach, but as Pancho came up beside Tim, he stopped his paddling to look back.

"Duck!" Tim commanded, and gasping in air,

they went under again. A moment later, they surfaced directly beneath the ladder.

"He's still going," Tim said, "but a lot slower. Bet he can't figure out where we are."

"Let's get aboard before he does," Pancho urged, starting up the ladder.

Tim climbed up swiftly behind him, and they had barely had time to duck below the rail when Rodrigo paused to look back again. This time the canoe glided to a stop, while his eyes searched the stretch of water between them.

"He's caught on that we aren't following him," Tim declared, as he peered over the rail. "He's liable to come back."

"Then we must get off the boat before he gets here. Quick! We will go below decks!"

Running in a crouch, the boys raced down the companion stairs. In the forepeak of the boat, more than two dozen bunks lay one above another in three tiers.

"It is here the fishermen will sleep," Pancho said. "But there will be many empty bunks."

"Which ones will be empty?"

"Who knows? I think the men are allowed to choose."

"Then we won't be safe in any of them." Tim bent down and opened a compartment beneath a lower bunk. Inside of it was an assortment of odds and ends. "What's this?"

"Just stowage space. If we could crawl in behind the junk, they wouldn't see us there."

"But we wouldn't see anything, either. Pancho," Tim asked with sudden realization, "if we hide down here, how can we see the pileup?"

"When it comes, we will hear shouting and run up."

"Then they'll catch us!"

"*Sí,* you are right," Pancho agreed thoughtfully. "This is not a good place to hide."

"Let's look up on deck," said Tim, leading the way, "but don't let Rodrigo see you."

At the top of the companionway, he turned and slipped into the galley. It was a large one, with booths along one side, and across the aisle from them, a counter with stools. Behind it were the cooking and refrigeration facilities.

"There's no place in here," Pancho declared, as he came in.

Tim was looking out toward the bay. Rodrigo, standing in his dugout just off the beach, seemed to be scrutinizing the decks of *La Hechicera.* While they watched, he dropped to his knees, and began to paddle toward the big boat.

"Wow! Now he's really suspicious!" Tim warned.

"*Sí!* We must find our hiding place, pronto!"

Together they slipped out onto the deck, taking care to stay below Rodrigo's line of vision. Abaft the galley, a hatch led down to the engine room. Behind that was a bait tank, and on the deck, nesting inside one another, were the skiffs. To try to hide in the top ones, beneath the protecting canvas, would be useless, for they would be lowered at the first fishing ground. Creeping forward to the bow, the boys found nothing but a hatch that led below to the chain locker.

"We could hide down there," Pancho offered, "but we would see nothing."

Atop the galley was the wheelhouse, and a ladder led from the deck to the bridge. Tim moved up one rung and again scanned the bay. Rodrigo was slicing

toward them, too intent on speed to look up. With a swift lunge, Tim reached the top of the ladder and slipped behind the railing. Followed by Pancho, he crept along the bridge to the aft end of the wheel-house, where two good-sized boxes offered some promise. Lifting a metal clasp, he peered inside the one nearest him. It was packed to the top with life belts.

"Maybe we could hide in there, if we took some of them out and stowed them below decks," Pancho suggested.

But Tim had already sighted a better possibility. On top of the wheelhouse was a lifeboat, inverted over two rafts.

"What's under that boat?" he asked.

"Boost me up, and I'll find out," Pancho ordered.

Sheltered from Rodrigo's view by the bulk of the wheelhouse, Tim pushed Pancho aloft, and he crawled around the side of the skiff. It was lashed down, but he managed to slip his arm between it and the rafts.

"There is nothing!"

"Could we get under it?"

"Sí—if we loosen this line. Tim, you have just had a great idea!" Pancho exulted. "We can lie flat on the rafts and be hidden by the boat over us. And on each side, there is space for us to peek out."

"And with the luck of The Sorceress," Tim declared jubilantly, "there will be no need for the lifeboat or the rafts. We'll be safe."

Pancho was peering over the top of the skiff. "If we are not caught now, by Rodrigo! I do not see his canoe. He must be tieing up alongside."

Pancho dropped to the bridge, and hastily, the boys swung down to the deck.

"Come on!" Pancho whispered, dashing forward to the bow. "While he comes up the ladder, we will go down the anchor chain."

Climbing onto the rail, Pancho grasped the big links in his hands and swung into space, with Tim right behind him. Inching down the chain, their arms strained by the hanging weight of their bodies, they descended slowly toward the water. When they were close enough to drop into it soundlessly, Pancho whispered, "Now—let go!"

With a small splash, they slid under and, rising to the surface, quickly filled their lungs. Then jackknifing, they dove into the graying depths and swam for their dugout.

When they came up alongside it, they could see Rodrigo's figure on the deck of *La Hechicera,* as he ran from stern to bow searching for them. Dusk was falling, and half obscured by the failing light, they climbed into the canoe. Dipping their paddles silently, they sliced away from the big boat.

They had gone some fifty yards before Rodrigo

spotted them. Lunging down the ladder, he untied his dugout and started after them, but they had beached their boat and were racing home when he touched shore.

"After supper, go for water to the spring," Pancho whispered as they ran. "I will meet you there and we will make plans."

Chapter Six

When the dishes had been washed and put away, Tim headed for the spring that bubbled out of the mountain just behind the village. Across his neck he wore a yoke from which two pails hung suspended, one on each end.

A few moments later, Pancho caught up with him. "I saw you go," he whispered, "but I was busy. Look!" He opened his shirt, and showed Tim a large flat package wrapped in a clean towel. "Tortillas and cheese," he confided. "I have smuggled out enough to feed us. Mariquita helped me."

"You mean you told her?" asked Tim, aghast.

"It is safe," Pancho assured him. "She is my sister —but she is also my friend. And tomorrow, she says, your father will be invited to the turtle barbecue, so he will not have to cook alone."

"Golly, that's great!" Tim exclaimed.

"Do you have the bag to keep the cheese and tortillas dry?"

"Sure—in our camping gear—and a thermos for drinking water. When do we go aboard?"

"As soon as everybody is asleep, we will swim out."

"Won't there be a man standing anchor watch on the boat?"

"*Sí*. We will need to watch him."

They had reached the spring, and as they filled their pails, they heard footsteps behind them.

"Don't say anything," Pancho warned. "I think Rodrigo has followed us!"

"What were you doing out by *La Hechicera?*" Rodrigo demanded, striding up to confront them.

"You saw us," Pancho replied easily, "we were swimming."

"That isn't all. You were on the boat. I'm going to tell my father."

"It was *you* who were on the boat," Pancho retorted. "We saw you."

"You were there before me," Rodrigo argued, "and whatever you were up to, I will find it out!"

Slipping under their yokes, the boys lifted their pails and balancing them carefully, headed back to the village, while the hostile Rodrigo lagged behind. As they reached the rear of the Ramirez house, Pancho handed the package of cheese and tortillas to Tim.

"Put it in the bag," he whispered, "and the water for drinking, too."

"I will," Tim promised. "D'you think Rodrigo will tell his father?"

"What has he to tell? He saw nothing—he was just fishing. But he is plenty suspicious, and if the idea of the stowing away should come to him—"

"What then?"

"He might go aboard early, with the anchor watch."

"Oh, boy, that's all we need!"

"It may be we can get there ahead of them."

"I can't go until my father's asleep."

"In my house there are more who must be asleep," Pancho reminded Tim, "but I will come out as soon as I can."

"Me, too."

Tim carried the two pails of water into the house and hid the package of food under his pillow. Earlier, he had secreted the thermos there, and some cookies in a waterproof bag. Now, while his father was still sitting outside by their campfire, would be his best chance to write the note he would leave on his pillow.

He tore a sheet of paper out of his school note-book and wrote the words that had been shaping in his mind:

> *Dear Dad,*
>   *Pancho and I are stowing away on* La He-chicera. *I have to see a spring pileup and*

*there's no other way. I hope you won't be
mad. You said I'd have an adventure and this
is it. Don't worry about me. I'll be safe.*

Tim
your compañero

He folded the paper and slipped it into the pocket
of his jeans. Then he went outside to join his father.
Every night they sat together by the campfire and
talked, while the gleaming red coals faded to embers,
and then they piled into bed.

It was the same with everybody in the village, except when the sport fishermen came. Then there was
the music of guitars and Mexican voices, singing.
Tonight five of the little planes had landed before
dark, and Tim could hear the music filtering down
from the other end of the settlement. It was a happy
sound, but it meant that everyone—including his
father and Pancho's family—would stay up later to
listen.

And the later they were, the more dangerous
would be the swim out to the charter boat, for the
rising moon was already sending a narrow path of
silver light across the bay. With each passing hour,
the path would become wider, until the whole bay
was one rippling sheet of silver. Then anyone looking across the water, whether from shore or from the
deck of *La Hechicera,* could easily spot two
swimmers.

The waiting—sitting there not able to share his feelings with his father—was nerve-wracking. He wanted to tell him everything, but he couldn't risk it. If his father knew about the stowing away, he'd have to forbid it, and that would be the end of the adventure. What happened afterwards—the severity of his punishment—didn't matter. The only important thing was to get away—get aboard and out past the island of the sea lions.

Tim felt as if his body were made of steel wires, all of them drawn so tightly that they were about to snap. And inside, there was a great empty hollow where his stomach should have been. He wasn't empty—he'd made himself eat, so he wouldn't be hungry on the boat. But if he'd been starving, he couldn't have felt more hollow. It was almost nauseating, and he wondered if what he felt was excitement—or fear.

He *was* scared, in a way. Scared of being stopped before they could get started, scared of being caught on board. But if that kind of fear could make him feel almost sick, what would happen to him if they really got into a pileup the way he wanted to—down in the water, in a skiff? Would he turn out to be a coward? If he did, everybody would see how it was with him—and tell his father. The thought made him sicker.

"Dad," he asked suddenly, "how does a person find out what he's like—*really*—inside of himself?"

"He begins by thinking, Son—by analyzing himself as honestly as if he were a stranger."

"But how do you do it? I mean, if there's some special thing you want to know about yourself."

"What special thing did you have in mind?"

"Well—like if a man wanted to know whether he was brave or a coward."

"I see," Mr. Allen said, thoughtfully. "Then I'd say the first thing he ought to think about is: what's the difference between the two? What would you say it is, Tim?"

"That's easy: a coward is scared and a brave man isn't."

"It's not quite that simple. There are many times when a brave man is afraid. That only means he has the sense to recognize danger when he sees it. It's what he does about it that makes the difference."

"You mean—like a coward runs away, and a brave man stays and fights?"

"That's it. But the fight doesn't have to be physical, Tim. Courage is a quality of mind. A courageous man is one who recognizes danger and faces it calmly and firmly, no matter what kind of danger it is."

"But what if he's never faced any kind, Dad? How can he know?"

"Chances are he has, Son, if he thinks about it. Take a boy like you, *mi compañero*: you can't think back to a time when you had to face a ferocious wild beast, because it's never happened to you—"

"That's what I mean."

"But you can think back to other situations that tested your courage."

"Like what, Dad?"

"Like when your mother died, Son. That's one of the most painful blows any boy ever has to take, and you took it with courage and helped me to go on making a life without her."

Tim was silent as he thought back to a year ago. The death of his mother had been the most painful thing that ever happened to him, and the hurt was still there. But he hadn't exactly thought of that as a test of courage.

"And you've probably faced dozens of other tests, Tim, without realizing it," his father went on. "Like, perhaps, a time when you stood up for a friend when everybody else was against him. A decision like that takes moral courage."

At the moment, Tim couldn't remember whether he'd ever made that sort of decision or not, and right now he didn't have time to search his memory. Instead, he thought about his father and the decision he had made when the other plane had collided with his jet.

"Dad—that time when you rode your jet out to sea, were you afraid?"

"You can bet I was, Tim, but I didn't have much

time to think about it. I was too busy trying to stay in the air long enough to get out beyond the city."

"You were thinking about all those people down under you," Tim said.

"You're right, Son, and I can tell you this: in a time of crisis, it helps a lot if you're thinking of somebody else, instead of yourself."

The red coals had faded to a pale pink, glowing faintly through the ashes, before Mr. Allen said, "Guess we'd better turn in, *mi compañero*. It's well past our bedtime."

It seemed to Tim that he had waited hours to hear those words. "You bet," he said, trying to sound as casual as if this were an ordinary night. "I sure am sleepy."

He kicked the sand onto the dying embers until they were thoroughly smothered and then followed his father into the little house. Undressing by the moonlight reflected from the sand outside, he slipped into his swimming trunks, and crawled into bed.

After he had said goodnight, he lay perfectly still, listening for the sound of his father's breathing. At first, he had to hold his own breath in order to hear it, but gradually the rhythm slowed, and it became more audible. When the long, deep pattern had remained unchanged for some time, he slipped from beneath the covers. Carefully drawing out the thermos and the bag of food from their hiding place, he put the note to his father on top of his pillow. Then he padded soundlessly out of the house.

Chapter Seven

Pancho had not yet come out, but at the other end of the beach the music had stopped and there were no lights in the cabins of the American fishermen. Apparently they, too, had gone to bed, for the crew would be taking them out to the charter boat at daybreak.

Tim looked at the bay. The path of moonlight had become a great shimmering highway, and in the center of it, silhouetted against the dazzle, was the dark shape of *La Hechicera,* riding at anchor. To reach her would be like swimming into a spotlight. And to cross the beach to the water would be dangerous, for a figure moving over the white sand would be almost as visible as by day.

Standing in the shadow of the palm-thatched *ramada,* Tim felt his heart pounding against his chest. There was still time to back out, to tear up the note and go back to bed. He could tell Pancho he had fallen asleep. But he knew he wouldn't. Whether he was brave or not, he wasn't that much of a coward.

Pancho emerged from the little house next door and beckoned to him, and together they moved to the outer fringe of the protecting shadows.

"It was hard to know when my mother was asleep," Pancho explained, in a soft whisper. "I could not come until I was sure."

"I wish I was sure everybody was asleep," Tim declared, uneasily. "If they aren't, we're in trouble already."

"*Si*—the moon is against us," Pancho agreed. "It may be we should not take the risk."

"Are you kidding?" Tim demanded. "Come on!"

Running in a low crouch, he crossed the moonlit sand and submerged himself shoulder deep in the water. Pancho waited a moment in the shadows and then followed him. Tim was strapping the water-proof bag containing the food and thermos to his waist as Pancho ducked in beside him, and together they surveyed the scene around them, giving particular attention to the house of Rodrigo and the dugouts in front of it. No figure emerged to challenge them.

"Okay," Tim whispered, *"this is it!"* He drew in a deep breath and started to push off, but Pancho stopped him.

"Wait! One more thing," he insisted. "We must swim slowly and try not to stir the water."

"Sure—I know," Tim said impatiently.

"No! It is not of the people that I am thinking. I have not wanted to scare you, but it is in the night that sharks come."

"Sharks?" Tim was stunned. "You mean they come into this bay at night?"

"*Si*, sometimes. They have a terrible hunger, and it is after the sun goes down that they search for food. In this bay there are seldom men in the water at night, but it is full of fish, and out by *La Hechicera* there will be eight or nine fathoms beneath us."

"Holy Smoke!" Tim whispered.

"I do not say that they *are* there, but it is possible. That is why we must swim without stirring the water. If there is a churning from our strokes, it will draw them to us."

Tim was silent. He hadn't counted on swimming in the dark through shark-infested waters.

"We can go back," Pancho suggested, "and nobody will even know we have been gone." He eyed the bay apprehensively. "I would just as soon go back."

"You knew about the sharks," Tim said, "and still you were willing to go."

"*Si*—willing," Pancho admitted weakly, "but I do not insist."

"You don't have to go," Tim said, after a moment, "but I'm going!"

"Then I, too!" Pancho declared staunchly.

When they had filled their lungs, they pushed off,

and with long, slow strokes swam just beneath the glittering surface. The light of the moon, slanting down into the water, illumined faintly the area just below them, and they saw hundreds of small shapes dart away in a swirl of confusion.

These were the harmless little fishes they saw every day, Tim reminded himself, but as the swift, shadowy bodies increased in size, he realized that the depth of the water was increasing too, and with it, the danger.

He surfaced for air, and Pancho came up beside him. They had covered no more than one fourth of the distance, and *La Hechicera* seemed very far away.

"It's hard to go so slow," Tim said.

"*Sí,* but from here on, it is even more important."

They went under, and as he swam, Tim peered through the silvery haze around him, fearful that he might see the dread outline of a shark with its high pectoral fin. But beyond the first few feet of palely luminous water, the blueness shaded into black, and he could see nothing.

Twice more he came up for air, and then jack-knifed beneath the silver dazzle to continue the long strokes that seemed so relaxed and easy, but were, in fact, becoming intolerable. Every nerve in his body screamed for speed, and he longed desperately to go thrashing toward the safety of the boat as fast as his arms and legs could take him.

Suddenly a large dark shape shot up toward him out of the depths, and he broke the surface with a cry of terror. But the water had entered his mouth muffling the sound, and choking, he fought to get his breath.

"It was not a shark!" Pancho's voice came from behind him. "I saw it—and I was afraid, but so was the fish. He went down quickly when you went up."

Tim gasped in the air and felt his pulse throbbing in his throat. "He touched my feet," he said, when he could speak.

"Look!" said Pancho. "We are almost there!"

Not more than twenty yards away *La Hechicera* rose high above them, flooded with moonlight. The danger from a man standing anchor watch on her decks was as nothing compared to the threat of a killer in the shimmering waters around them.

Tim felt a strong, almost uncontrollable impulse to race to her side and knew that Pancho felt it with him, but speed could still be their undoing. Suddenly he remembered that his father had said courage was the ability to face danger calmly and firmly.

"Go slow!" he warned Pancho, and together they stroked carefully across the final stretch of water.

A skiff was tied alongside, in the shadow of the big boat, and they climbed into it, grateful to be safely out of the reach of predators. But its presence told them that there was a man on board—and possibly with him, Rodrigo.

When they had rested and let the water drip from their bodies, they climbed up the ladder and peered cautiously over the rail. They could see no one on deck, but in the galley, illumined by the light of one lamp, a man was moving around.

"Wait here!" Pancho whispered, and slipping over the rail, he crept across the deck for a closer view; then he motioned Tim to follow him.

As he reached Pancho's side, Tim saw that the man in the galley was Catarino, the deckhand with whom they had carried the striped marlin up the beach on that first day. There was no sign of Rodrigo. Catarino was pouring himself a cup of coffee, and as they watched, he moved around the end of the bar to sit down—facing them—to drink it. Instantly, both of them ducked.

"When he finishes the coffee, he may come out on deck," Pancho whispered. "We must get to the bridge before then."

Crouching below the level of the galley windows, they moved silently to the ladder that took them to the bridge and ascended it swiftly. They were abreast the wheelhouse when Tim thought he saw something moving inside of it. He dropped to his knees and instinctively, Pancho followed suit.

"There's someone in there!" Tim whispered.

"Rodrigo!" Pancho concluded.

Hardly daring to breathe, they waited in suspense for him to come out, but nothing happened.

"Maybe he did not see us," Pancho ventured at last, "but if he is there, we cannot get to the lifeboat."

Tim realized it was true. The wheelhouse was glassed in, all around; in this moonlight, they could not possibly climb up on top of it without being seen by anyone inside. And to hide below decks, they'd have to get back down before Catarino came out of the galley.

"Maybe you imagined you saw something," Pancho suggested.

Tim inched up to peer into the wheelhouse, and when he said nothing, Pancho came up beside him. Abaft the helm, there were four bunks for the use of the skipper and his crew, and on one of them, clearly visible in the moonlight, lay Rodrigo. As they stared, he turned over toward them, and they saw that he was asleep.

"So he did come," Tim breathed.

"But he could not stay awake till we got here!" Pancho grinned with delight. "Let's go aloft, while we can."

Moving with great care, lest they disturb the sleeper, Tim hoisted Pancho topside of the wheelhouse and was in turn hauled up after him. Catarino was still in the galley, but he might appear at any minute. Only one obstacle remained, now, between them and their hiding place underneath the lifeboat: the lashing lines that held the little boat and rafts secure against the rolling of *La Hechicera*.

They attacked the knots immediately, but the lines had been tied by hands stronger than theirs, and they could not loosen them. Desperately, they continued to struggle while keeping a lookout for Catarino.

At length one knot gave way, and they were able to lift the little boat just enough to wriggle under one side. Unfastening the waterproof bag from around his waist, Tim pushed it under and worked his way in after it. When Pancho had squirmed in beside him, he retied the knot. The line was less tight, but they could only hope that no one would notice it.

Pulling the little skiff down to its former position on the rafts, they collapsed in relief. They had made it. For the present, they were safe.

Inverted over them, the lifeboat was like a small black cave, with just a few inches of opening on each side, where its gunwale curved up from the rafts. Through this opening they could peer out when they chose, but now, exhausted from the prolonged strain of their adventure, they lay still and were soon as soundly asleep as their antagonist in the wheelhouse beneath them.

The roar of outboard motors woke them. It was barely daybreak, but already the men of the crew were bringing the American fishermen aboard. Alert with excitement, Tim and Pancho lay on their sides in the narrow confinement of their hiding place, heads flat to the canvas so that each could peer out through the small opening between raft and skiff.

They could see very little of the deck of *La Hechicera,* but beyond her they viewed a portion of the bay and the motor-powered skiffs racing toward her, their foaming white wakes fanning out behind them. One by one, the motors were cut off, and the mingling of Mexican and American voices told the boys that crew and fishermen had come aboard.

From a ventilator in the galley, the tantalizing aroma of fresh coffee wafted up on the morning air, and they became uncomfortably aware of hunger pangs, but they decided to ignore them until the boat was safely underway. Below decks, her motors were warming up, and the rattle of the big iron chain indicated that the crew was getting up the anchor.

The waters of the bay were taking on the flame tints of the sunrise when the boys felt the motion of the boat.

"She is underway!" Pancho whispered.

The little fleet of skiffs and cruisers riding at anchor began to recede gradually as *La Hechicera* crept slowly out of the harbor, and Tim thought, *Now it has really begun!*

The charter boat was well out into the channel that separated the coast of Baja from the offshore islands before the boys permitted themselves to eat. Unzipping the waterproof bag, Tim doled out a small portion of tortillas and cheese to each of them, and they ate slowly, to make it last longer. With so small a supply of food and water, they knew they would have to ration it carefully.

They were still hungry when Tim placed the package of food back in the bag and lifted out the thermos. Unscrewing the cap, he poured a small amount into each of the two green plastic cups. As they drank the water, they were startled to hear the voice of Rodrigo at very close range.

"He must be on the bridge!" Pancho whispered.

"Listen!" Tim warned.

Rodrigo's words came up to them clearly. "Catarino," he was saying, "if somebody wanted to stow away on this boat, where would be the best place to hide?"

In tense anxiety, the boys waited for his answer.

"You know of somebody who wants to stow away?" Catarino asked.

"It is just a game," Rodrigo replied evasively, "to think of all the good places."

"*Sí?*" There was a pause; then Catarino suggested, "How about one of the bunks below decks?"

"I have thought of that; it is too easy."

"That means he's already looked there!" Pancho whispered.

"Then," Catarino went on, "have you thought of the anchor-chain locker?"

"No. That is a good one!"

From somewhere below, a voice called, "Rodrigo! Come down, pronto!"

"You had better get down to the galley," Catarino warned, "or it is you who will need the hiding place!"

There was no further conversation, and the boys guessed that Rodrigo had gone back to his job.

"He'll look in the anchor-chain locker the first chance he gets," Tim whispered.

"*Sí*, and when he does not find us there, he will come back, and Catarino will think of another place."

"Maybe this one," Tim declared. Automatically, he was starting to screw the cap back on the thermos. "Give me your cup," he said.

"My cup?" Pancho fumbled for it in the semi-darkness, but his search yielded nothing. Peering under the gunwale, he discovered that it had rolled out onto the very edge of the wheelhouse.

"Now I have done it!" he moaned. "If I stretch out my arm, and somebody is looking, we are finished! And I think even if I took the risk, it is beyond my reach."

Tim tightened the cap that was the larger of the cups and then flattened himself to peek out. The small cup lay definitely beyond their reach, a bright green signpost pointing straight to their hiding place.

"How much time have we got, before we get to the island of the sea lions?" Tim asked.

"It is hard to say," Pancho whispered, "but I think

it may be we will come to it soon."

"Rodrigo will search till he finds us," Tim asserted, "but if Alfaro keeps him busy long enough in the galley—"

"*Sí,* and if nobody sees the green cup!"

"Do you think we'll be able to see the island of the sea lions from here?" Tim asked, as he lay peering out at the water.

"If we do not see it, we will hear it," Pancho told him.

Taut with apprehension, the boys waited, listening for the sound of Rodrigo's voice—or the barking that would tell them they were approaching the island— but only the voices of crew and fishermen floated up to them from the decks below, while the delicious fragrance of tortillas and beans assaulted them from the galley.

The sun was climbing higher, sending its hot rays down onto the little skiff that curved over them, and the narrow stretch of sea within their view seemed to lengthen out interminably, as *La Hechicera* pushed through the gentle swell of the channel.

Then, very faintly, they heard a far-off muttering.

"It is the sea lions!" Pancho whispered excitedly.

Gradually, as the boat drew nearer, the muttering became a clamorous barking and roaring from hundreds of lusty throats. The island swam into view, and Tim saw that it was a barren mass of volcanic rock rising up out of the ultramarine blue of the sea.

Its pinnacles were plastered white with guano, and
above them, countless seabirds were circling and
shrieking, but it was the blatant creatures sprawled
on the shelves of rock that the boys were straining
to see.

Several hundred of them were congregated together in noisy confusion, while scores more were
already sliding off the sloping ledges to come trum-
peting out toward the boat. They were huge, tawny
fellows with mustaches, and as they approached *La
Hechicera,* they trod water and bellowed at the
intruders.

"Holy Smoke!" Tim whispered, in awe. "I hope

79

we don't get thrown into the water with them!"

He made an effort to hear any sound of Rodrigo over the uproar and kept the little green plastic cup in view. If anyone picked that up, before they were past the island . . . A cold chill ran down his spine at the thought, and he waited in breathless suspense as the charter boat sailed slowly past the chorus of bulls.

Chapter Eight

They had left the island far behind and were sailing south on a flat-calm sea when a shout came from the wheelhouse below them.

"Pileup to starboard!"

"Pileup!" Tim echoed, in an awed whisper. "Pancho—it's happening!"

The excited voices of crew and fishermen passed the word, and there was a sound of running feet on the decks. Instantly both boys flattened themselves face down to peer out through the narrow space beneath the gunwale.

"I can't see anything!" Tim whispered, in distress. "Where is it?"

"This space is too small," said Pancho. "It must be happening in a place beyond where we can see."

"Then we've got to make *more* space!" Grasping

the gunwale with both hands, Tim pushed upward, but the heavy skiff lifted no more than an inch or two. "Help me!" he commanded.

Pancho added his strength to the lifting, but still they could see no sign of the pileup. "There is no way, unless we loosen the lines," he sighed regretfully.

"Then let's loosen them!"

"But if I put out my hands to untie them, someone may see me."

"With all that's going on, nobody'll be looking!" Tim insisted.

On the bridge, the captain was barking out orders. As *La Hechicera* hove to, Pancho lay on his side, preparing to reach out toward the lines.

"I will do it," he said, "but it is a big risk we take."

"If we *don't* take it, then all the rest was for nothing," Tim protested, his voice rising urgently. "The pileup is happening out there, right now, and we're missing it!"

"S-sh!" Pancho hissed suddenly.

Startled into silence, Tim waited while Pancho lay motionless, peering out. "What is it?" he whispered, after a moment. When Pancho made no answer, Tim started to edge toward the small opening, but the free arm of his friend stopped him.

"Don't move!" Pancho warned, in a barely audible

82

whisper. "It is Rodrigo. When you spoke loud, he heard your voice, but he does not yet know where it came from."

"Is he looking this way?"

"*Si*—right at the skiff over our heads."

"Then he'll see—"

"—the cup!" Pancho cut in. "He sees it now!"

In an instant, Rodrigo had fitted the two clues together. "Stowaways!" he yelled exultantly. "Papa! Papa! Look here! There are stowaways, and I have found them!"

There was a pause in the loud flow of orders. "Stowaways!" the captain muttered unbelievingly. "Don't bother me with nonsense!"

"But Papa, it is true!" Rodrigo insisted. "They are there, under the skiff. I know it by the green cup!"

The captain spoke a low command, there was an answering murmur from inside the wheelhouse, and then a hand reached up to take the cup. A moment later, a pair of hands became visible as they untied the lashing lines.

Hardly breathing, the boys waited for the awful moment of discovery.

"*Santa Madre,* help us!" Pancho whispered softly.

The hands on the knots were strong and swift, the lines fell away, and the little sheltering cave of the lifeboat was rudely lifted, exposing the stowaways.

Catarino, who had uncovered them, stared in

amazement. *"Nombre de a Santo!"* he exclaimed. "You were right, Rodrigo!"

El Capitán stood on the bridge, glaring up at them. He was a big, heavy-set man, and with his swarthy skin and large bushy *mostacho,* he looked to Tim exactly like a pirate.

"Caramba!" he boomed. "Bring them down to me!"

"Vamos—pronto!" Catarino ordered, prodding them a little.

While they were swinging down, the captain was cross-examining Rodrigo sharply.

"And you, *mi hijo,"* he was saying, "how is it that *you* have found them?"

"I heard a voice, and then I saw the green cup."

"You saw more!" the captain insisted. "And *I* see it now: it was because of them you wanted to come aboard with Catarino last night!"

"I saw nothing," Rodrigo replied uneasily, "I only suspected."

"And if you suspected, why did you not tell me? Out at sea is not the place to find stowaways. Last night, anchored in the bay—that was the place!"

Catarino was shoving Tim and Pancho along the bridge toward the captain, and he turned to glower at them.

"What is it that you are doing here?" he demanded angrily. "Why did you stow away on this boat?"

84

Struck dumb by the big rumble of his voice and the fierce pirate look of him, the boys made no answer. Below, on the decks, the rushing and shouting continued as the fishermen scrambled to get their gear, and the crew worked at lowering the outboard skiffs. Tim longed to look toward the scene of excitement, but he didn't dare take his eyes from the captain's.

"Por Dios, you will answer me, or I will feed you to the fishes!" he was roaring at them.

Pancho, who had witnessed *El Capitán's* wrath on other occasions, finally managed to speak. "It was I who had the idea, *Señor Capitán."*

Tim found his voice quickly. "No, *Señor*—it was my idea. I wanted to see a spring pileup!"

"A pileup!" the captain snorted. "Do you think, on this charter for the game fishermen, I have room in the skiffs for stowaway boys?"

"No, sir—but I had no other way," Tim ventured. "I have no money, and soon I'll be going home. If I don't see this pileup now, I may never have another chance. Please, sir—"

"And you," the captain cut in, scowling at Pancho, "I suppose you will not have another chance!"

"For me, there will be the chance, *Señor Capitán,"* Pancho admitted, "but Tim is my friend. I could not let him go alone."

"You will not need to worry. He will not go alone

where I will send him. You will go with him—and Rodrigo, too!"

"But Papa!" Rodrigo protested.

"*Silencio!*" the captain commanded. "Catarino, before you go to your skiff, you will take them below decks and lock them up. And there they will stay until I have decided on their punishment."

"Please, *Señor Capitán,*" Tim pleaded, "I'll work hard. I'll do *anything* if you'll just let me stay on deck and watch the pileup!"

"No! There will be no pileup for stowaways!" the captain declared with finality. "Take them below, pronto!"

Catarino had just climbed down the ladder to the deck, followed by the three boys, when a crewman shouted, "Catarino—*vamos*! Your boat is ready!"

"Then you take them below!" he ordered as he hurried over the rail.

In the confusion, the boys were momentarily forgotten, and they snatched their chance to look for the pileup. A half-mile away, one spot in the smooth blue of the water seemed to be bubbling and foaming, as if a hot spring were gushing up from the bottom. While they gazed in fascination, the convulsions increased, and there were flashes of silver spewed up by the commotion beneath. Overhead, the seabirds were already winging in to circle and dive in shrieking contention.

Standing at the rail as the first skiffs roared off,

Tim felt an agony of longing. If only he were in one of them!

Behind him, an American fisherman, racing along the deck, slowed down just long enough to whisper, "Jump overboard, Son, and we'll pick you up!"

Tim stared in astonishment as the man ran on to swing over the rail and down the ladder toward the skiff waiting beneath him. On the bridge, the captain was again barking out orders, when his glance came to rest on the three boys. With a commanding gesture, he directed them to go below.

Tim made a quick decision. Climbing over the rail, he dropped into the sea. In amazement, Pancho looked from the captain to Tim, and then, as the busy crewman ran forward to stop him, he followed his friend. Not anxious to face his father's wrath alone, Rodrigo plunged in after them.

While the skipper thundered his protest from the bridge, the boys swam frantically toward the skiff, to be swiftly hauled inboard by the Americans.

Already in the boat, as their Mexican guide, was Catarino. "Santo Dios!" he exclaimed, in dismay. "Now he will kill us, all four!"

"Come on, let's go!" one of the Americans commanded.

With a yank, Catarino started the motor, and the skiff roared off after the others.

The threat of the punishment that lay ahead dropped quickly out of Tim's mind in the excite-

ment of the moment. Seven outboards were racing toward the pileup, and he and Pancho were in one of them!

Crouching beside him, Pancho shouted over the roar, "It is as I told you—*La Hechicera* has brought us the luck!"

Ahead of them, the upheaval was still expanding, as though a hundred separate springs had boiled up, spreading their turbulent waters until there was no smooth surface left anywhere. Thousands of glistening bodies shimmered in the sunlight, as the forage

fishes leapt above the sea to escape the greedy game
fish below. And signalled by the screaming of the
first seabirds, hundreds of gulls and terns, boobies
and frigates and pelicans were zooming in to add to
the deafening tumult.

The American anglers had taken positions facing
the rear and let out their lines for trolling, but the
three boys were crouched in the bow of the boat,
viewing the scene with mingled excitement and un-
easiness. As the skiff sped into the midst of the tur-
moil, the waters seemed to explode into new violence.

Great schools of ravenous migrators were spurting after sardines and herrings and gold-striped grunt.

Tim recognized the streamlined yellowtails, the cabrillas with the large reddish-brown spots, the big skipjacks with the dark stripes on their bellies, the threadfin pompanos, the yellow jack crevalles with their blunt heads, the brilliant red bodies of the ruby snappers. Scores of other varieties, small and large, striped and spotted, churned around them in a swimming rainbow of colors.

On the island of the sea lions, the cries of the birds had stirred the big mammals, and they were already coursing in, announcing their arrival with a hubbub of barks and bellows. Pods of porpoises, alerted by their own built-in sonar systems, were humping their backs and beating their tails to speed in great arching jumps toward the melee.

There was a thrilling beauty in the multitude of leaping, shining bodies, but there was a terrible savagery, too, in the crazed slaughter of one fish by another, in the blood-stained waters. And then, suddenly, the scene became more frightening as the great monsters appeared from the depths—the two-hundred pound baya groupers, the black sea bass, nearly three times as large, the gigantic thousand-pound *meros,* their huge, gaping mouths big enough to take in the body of a man.

Tim's heart was pounding furiously, and again he felt the strong pulse-beat in his throat as he watched the uproar around him. In all seven skiffs, the anglers had big hookups, and the guides were maneuvering the outboards through the murderous waters, while the men worked their fish. The air was thick with the wheeling and diving of birds, the frenzied leaps of fishes, fleeing and pursuing, as though every sea creature had gone wild. And then, for the first time, Tim saw the grim dorsal fin of a shark, as the beast cruised with incredible speed toward the fracas. Slashing and biting at everything that moved before him, he sliced between the boats, revealing his grotesque T-shaped head, with an eye at each tip.

"The *cornuda!*" Pancho cried, in alarm.

Threshing the water as he gutted a grouper, the twelve-foot monster made a fast turn, using his ugly hammerhead as a rudder, and in passing, he grazed the bow of the skiff. The little boat rocked from the impact, and the boys clung to the gunwale in horror, aware that the thousand-pound bulk of the shark might easily have spilled them into the sea. Shaken and trembling from the encounter, they watched as the fearsome killer cut away to gorge himself in another part of the pileup.

It was then that the hookup of the friendly American caught their attention. At the end of his line, a magnificent sailfish broke through the surface to lunge upward in a flying leap, the bluish-purple of his great dorsal fin rising like a sail along his back.

In the same instant, a big golden fish with a high, blunt forehead took off in a bounding jump right over the skiff. Tim glimpsed him coming, out of the corner of his eye, and ducked—but Pancho, excited by the tail-walking acrobatics of the sailfish, stood up just in time to be hit by the blunt head and slammed overboard. The *dorado* continued on his way, while Pancho, knocked unconscious by the driving blow, sank under the churning waters.

Tim saw him disappear and screamed for help, but a barking seal drowned out his cry, and the full attention of both boatman and anglers was focused on their fishing. He turned to Rodrigo and saw that he was frozen with terror. There could be no help from him. Already the skiff had moved away from the spot where Pancho had gone down. In another instant, it would be lost to sight, and Pancho's unconscious body abandoned to the killers.

There was no time to think. With one more desperate yell for help, Tim plunged into the bloody waters and swam back through the slippery, milling bodies. Reaching what he thought was the place where his friend had disappeared, he jackknifed under. There was no sign of Pancho.

Coming up for air, he scanned the seething melee of fishes. Suddenly, as though propelled from beneath by a playful porpoise, Pancho was lifted above the sea, some twenty feet away.

Swiftly, Tim stroked toward him and grasped him

in his arms. Treading water, he held him above the surface. All around them, the nightmarish massacre continued, but on the skiff, Rodrigo had pulled out of his paralysis to command the attention of Catarino, and the outboard was circling back.

Moments later, the Americans had hauled them into the boat and were expertly reviving Pancho, while in the other skiffs, anglers and guides now aware of the rescue, were shouting, *"Bravo, Timo! Viva Pancho! Viva Timo! Bravo, bravo!"*

Back on *La Hechicera*, there was still the wrathful captain to face, but before he could pass sentence on the boys, the sport fishermen and crew interceded. When he had been told of Pancho's narrow escape and Tim's courageous rescue, he relented.

"For so brave and good a friend as Timo, there should be a reward," the captain declared, "and it shall be this: that for him and his *amigo,* there shall be no punishment."

"Rodrigo helped," Tim said. "It was he who made them see us and come back."

"Sí—you have both done well," the captain agreed. "And now you have learned the danger. For this, I did not want to risk you in the skiffs. I might have had to sail home and tell two fathers that their sons were lost in the sea. I am glad it is not so, and I can, instead, tell to the father of Timo that he has for son, a *héroe!"*

"*Sí*. He will be *mucho orgulloso!*" Catarino promised.

"It means he will be very proud," Pancho translated, "and for me, too, it is true. You have saved my life, *amigo,* and I am proud to have such a friend."

"But for me, you wouldn't have been there," Tim reminded him. "You took a lot of risks."

"*Sí,*" Pancho agreed, with a grin, "we are *two* good friends!" He looked at Rodrigo, who smiled at them awkwardly. "And I think, now, maybe three!"

For the rest of the voyage, the boys were privileged to sleep in the bunks below decks and eat the fine Mexican cooking of Alfaro, in the galley. And as the boat sailed through the deep blue waters of the Cortez, Tim saw more of the great creatures of the sea: a pair of rapacious killer whales, and a herd of the eighty-foot finbacks; the enormous manta rays, flapping their twenty-foot width through the water or soaring high above it; the deadly requiem sharks, the dazzling, fighting black marlins, and pods of wonderful, smiling, bottle-nosed dolphins.

All these and more he saw from the safety of *La Hechicera*'s decks, but he knew he would never forget the exciting and frightening hour in the heart of the pileup. He *had* been scared, and he had learned that what his father said was true: there had been no time to worry about being afraid; thinking of Pancho had made him forget everything else. That had made all the difference.